JEFFERSON COUNTY LIBRARY
620 Cedar Avenue
Port Hadlock, WA 98339
(360) 385-6544   www.jclibrary.info

Saddle Bronc Riding

By John Hamilton

Visit us at
www.abdopublishing.com

Published by ABDO Publishing Company, PO Box 398166, Minneapolis, MN 55439. Copyright ©2014 by Abdo Consulting Group, Inc. International copyrights reserved in all countries. No part of this book may be reproduced in any form without written permission from the publisher. A&D Xtreme™ is a trademark and logo of ABDO Publishing Company.

Printed in the United States of America, North Mankato, Minnesota.
052013
092013

 PRINTED ON RECYCLED PAPER

Editor: Sue Hamilton
Graphic Design: John Hamilton
Cover: John Hamilton
Photos: All photos by John Hamilton, except: Tom Baker-pg 26; Library of Congress-pg 6-7.

ABDO Booklinks
Web sites about rodeos are featured on our Book Links pages. These links are routinely monitored and updated to provide the most current information available. Web site: www.abdopublishing.com

Library of Congress Control Number: 2013931682

Cataloging-in-Publication Data

Hamilton, John.
 Saddle bronc riding / John Hamilton.
  p. cm. -- (Xtreme rodeo)
ISBN 978-1-61783-980-1
1. Bronc riding--Juvenile literature. I. Title.
791.8/4--dc23

                    2013931682

Contents

Saddle Bronc Riding

Saddle bronc riding is the classic rodeo event. It pits one cowboy on a saddle versus a bucking, spine-jarring tornado of horse energy. When a skilled cowboy rides a good bucking horse, he and the horse get into a beautiful rhythm.

The cowboy matches his movements with the horse's best efforts to toss him to the ground. A great saddle bronc ride is like watching poetry in motion.

History

In the mid-1800s, during the days of the North American Old West, ranch hands gathered and competed. They wanted to see who had the best style when it came to riding untamed horses. The first official rodeo competition may have been held as early as 1869 in Deer Trail, Colorado.

Today, the Professional Rodeo Cowboys Association (PRCA) sanctions more than 600 rodeos in 37 states and 3 Canadian provinces.

"Rodeo" is a Spanish word used by early cowboys when they gathered up their cattle. The English translation is "round up."

Rules

Saddle bronc rides start in a small pen called a bucking chute. When the cowboy is mounted in the saddle and ready, he raises his free hand, nods his head, and the gate is opened. That's when the bucking action begins. A full ride lasts for eight seconds. The cowboy must hang on to a braided rein using only one hand. His free hand must be kept in the air. If he touches the horse or his own body or equipment, the judges give him a no-score.

Marking Out

Before the bronc makes its first jump out of the bucking chute, the rider must have both spurs touching above the horse's shoulders. This is called "marking out." The rider must keep the spurs in this position until after the horse's feet hit the ground. This gives the horse an advantage. If the cowboy fails to mark out, he is disqualified.

Spurring Action

To receive a high score, the saddle bronc rider demonstrates he's in control during even the wildest ride.

When the horse bucks, the cowboy pulls his knees up and rolls his spurs along the horse's shoulders. When the horse comes down, he tries to straighten his legs, toes pointed out, above the horse's shoulders. A good ride is like a fluid dance, with the cowboy reacting and adjusting to every bone-rattling buck and twist.

Bucking spurs are blunt and turn freely. They do not hurt the horses, which have very thick hides.

Scoring

Saddle bronc riding is a rough stock event. Scores are based on the performance of the rider and the animal. Two judges each give the cowboy a score ranging from 1 to 25 points. Cowboys who have smooth rides with good spurring action get higher scores. Instead of brute strength, saddle bronc riders rely on timing, grace, and rhythm. A good ride appears to be effortless, but great skill is required.

Each judge also gives the bronc a score of 1 to 25 points. High-scoring broncs give powerful rides, with lots of high-kicking action. At the end of the ride, the two judges add their scores, for a total possible of 100 points. A total score in the high 80s is considered a good ride.

Equipment

Saddle bronc riders require special saddles. They can cost $1,500 or more. They are lightweight, with no saddle horn in front that would injure the cowboy. Leather stirrups move freely so the cowboy can have better spurring action. Cowboys hang on to a thick, braided rope called a hack rein with one hand. The hack rein is attached to a halter on the bronc's head.

Cowboys use similar saddles called "association saddles," which have regulated measurements and modifications for fairness.

Chaps protect the legs from hooves or flying clods of dirt. Decorative fringe on the chaps give more "movement" to a ride.

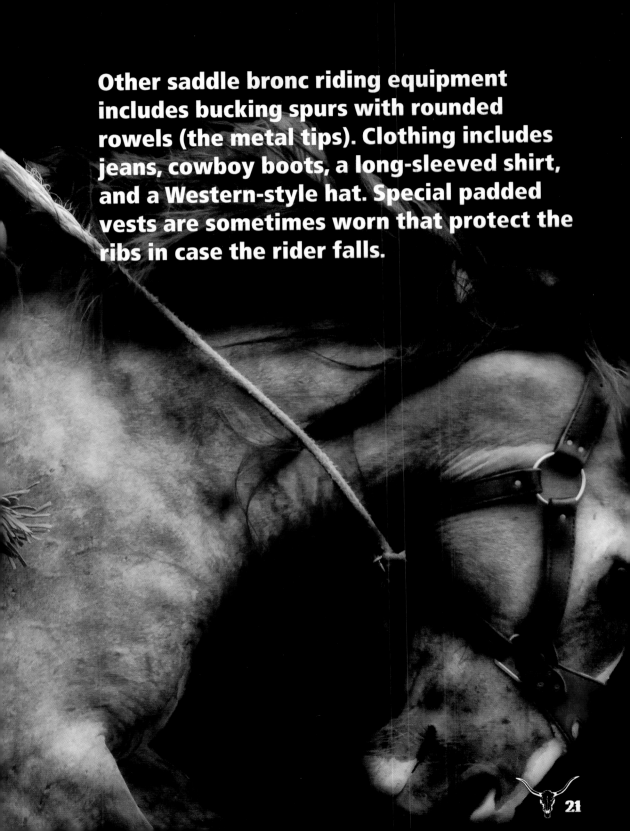

Other saddle bronc riding equipment includes bucking spurs with rounded rowels (the metal tips). Clothing includes jeans, cowboy boots, a long-sleeved shirt, and a Western-style hat. Special padded vests are sometimes worn that protect the ribs in case the rider falls.

Pickup Men

The pickup man is the rodeo cowboy's best friend. In saddle bronc riding and bareback riding, when the eight-second ride is over, sometimes the horse just keeps on bucking, or heads in the wrong direction away from the exit.

The pickup man swoops in, helping transfer the cowboy safely off the runaway horse. It's a dangerous moment. Pickup men have great horsemanship, timing, and guts.

Injuries

Saddle bronc riding is a dangerous sport. If a cowboy gets bucked off his ride, he can suffer broken bones, bruises, and concussions. Getting "dashboarded" is when a cowboy is thrown over the front of his horse. Trampling is always a danger. Trained paramedics are an important part of any rodeo. Rodeo cowboys are a tough breed, but it's always good to have help on hand when you need it.

Horses

Rodeo horses are specially bred. Top saddle broncs are prized for their agility, strength, and especially their natural ability to buck. They are untamed, which makes them too dangerous for activities like ranching or racing. But they are perfect for rodeos.

Saddle broncs are larger and more sturdy than bareback riding horses. The best broncs have rodeo careers that last for many years.

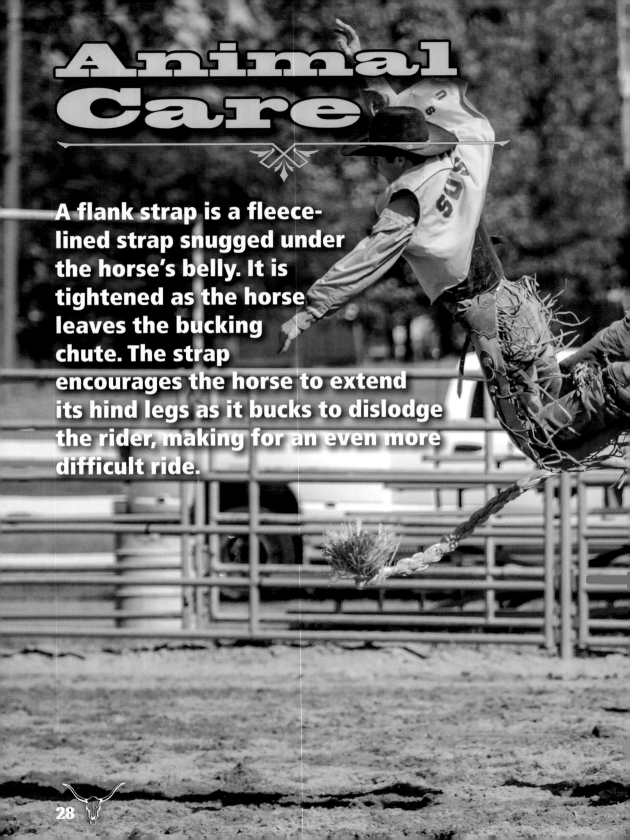

Animal Care

A flank strap is a fleece-lined strap snugged under the horse's belly. It is tightened as the horse leaves the bucking chute. The strap encourages the horse to extend its hind legs as it bucks to dislodge the rider, making for an even more difficult ride.

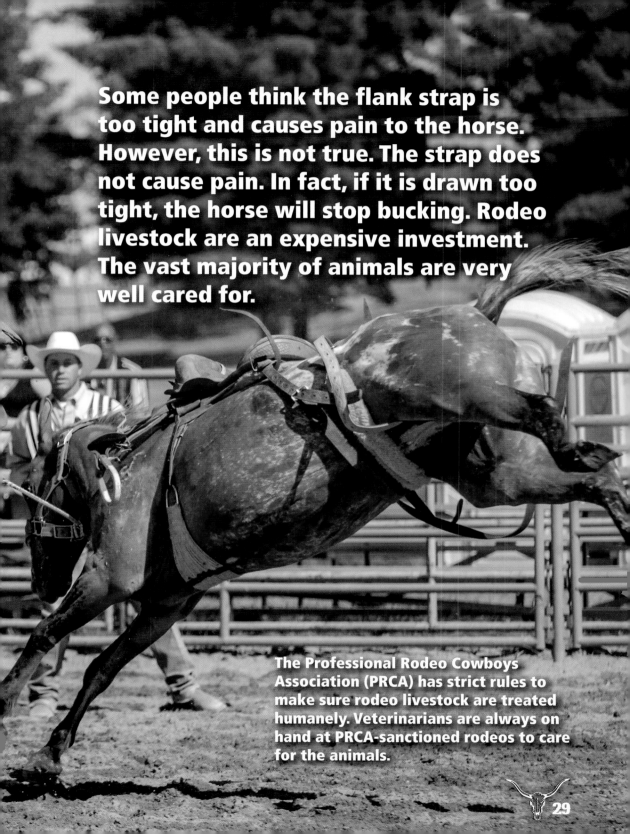

Some people think the flank strap is too tight and causes pain to the horse. However, this is not true. The strap does not cause pain. In fact, if it is drawn too tight, the horse will stop bucking. Rodeo livestock are an expensive investment. The vast majority of animals are very well cared for.

The Professional Rodeo Cowboys Association (PRCA) has strict rules to make sure rodeo livestock are treated humanely. Veterinarians are always on hand at PRCA-sanctioned rodeos to care for the animals.

Glossary

Chaps

Leather or suede leg coverings. They are buckled on over trousers. Working cowboys use chaps while riding on horseback through heavy brush. Rodeo chaps are colorful and have a lot of fringe. The flapping fringe makes a ride seem even more exciting.

Flank Strap

A fleece-covered leather strap that is secured with a buckle and snugged under a horse or bull's belly near the sensitive flank area. It encourages them to extend their rear legs, but does not cause pain.

Free Hand

Bareback, saddle bronc, and bull riders can hang on with only one hand. Their free hand must not touch the animal or themselves, or they are disqualified.

Hack Rein
A long, thick, braided rein that is attached to a halter on the horse's head. A bit is not used because it would harm the horse. The cowboy holds onto the hack rein with one hand. Also called a bronc rein.

Marking Out
During the saddle bronc's first jump out of the chute, the cowboy's spurs must touch the top of the animal's shoulders.

Professional Rodeo Cowboys Association
The PRCA is the largest and oldest rodeo sanctioning organization in the world. It ensures that rodeos meet high standards in working conditions and livestock welfare. Located in Colorado Springs, Colorado, it sanctions about 600 rodeos in the United States and Canada.

Rough Stock
Untamed horses and bulls.

Index

Paige Oveson, Miss Rodeo Minnesota 2011.